Black, White, Just Right!

Marguerite W. Davol

illustrated by **Irene Trivas**

ALBERT WHITMAN & COMPANY, CHICAGO, ILLINOIS

Library of Congress Cataloging-in-Publication Data
Davol, Marguerite W.
Black, white, just right!/Marguerite W. Davol;
illustrated by Irene Trivas.
p. cm.
Summary: A girl explains how her parents are
different in color, have different tastes in art, food,
and pets, and how she herself is different too,
but just right.
[1. Individuality—Fiction 2. Interracial
marriage—Fiction. 3. Parent and child—Fiction.]
1. Trivas, Irene, ill. II. Title.
PZ7.D32114B1 1993   93-19932
[E]-dc20   CIP
                                                      AC

Printed in China
14 13 12 11 10 9 NP 20 19 18 17 16 15

Illustrations rendered in gouache
Text type set in Veljovic Medium
Calligraphy by Robert Borja

For more information about Albert Whitman & Company,
visit our web site at www.albertwhitman.com.

For my just-right grandchildren, Stephen and Nicole. M.W.D.

Mama's face is chestnut brown.
Her dark brown eyes are bright as bees.
Papa's face turns pink in the sun;
his blue eyes squinch up when he smiles.

My face? I look like both of them—
a little dark, a little light.
Mama and Papa say, "Just right!"

Black is the color of Mama's hair,
crinkly, curling around her face.
Papa's hair is popcorn colored,
short and straight and silky-smooth.

My hair? Halfway in-between—
a dark brown ponytail tied tight.
Three in the mirror—we look just right!

Mama and I take ballet lessons,
twirling, leaping, light as moths.

Papa likes to dance to rap,
stomp and wiggle to the street-smart beat.

My feet? They never want to stop!
I'm Papa's jitterbug—boom, bamty, boom!
I'm Mama's butterfly—arms wide in flight.
We all clap and say, "Just right!"

When Mama walks along the street,
her high-heeled shoes click click—fast.
Papa likes to dawdle, stroll,
make faces in the window glass.

My speed? I race like a rabbit,
then let my toes drag turtle-slow.
Mama sighs. "We don't have all night!"
Swift or slow, I say, "Just right!"

Mama says, "I'd like a kitten,
plump and gray, all fur and purr."

Papa wants a Saint Bernard—
too bad that we don't have a yard!

And me? Give me dozens of pets:
cats and dogs, flat fish, fat frogs.
I'd make sure they didn't fight.
A whole pet store would be just right!

Mama stares at African masks,
curved drums, carved figures made of wood.

Papa goes for modern art,
all squiggles, squares, and stretched-out shapes.

My choice? Huge Egyptian tombs,
with painted faces, picture words,
and cloth-wrapped mummies wound up tight.
Touring the museum is just right!

Mama orders vegetables,
fruit and yogurt for dessert.
Barbequed ribs are Papa's choice,
bagels, beans, blueberry pie.
My meal? Why not try it all?
I'm Mama and Papa's Bottomless Pit.
I clean my plate, beg, "One more bite!"
Patting my stomach, I say, "Just right!"

Mama has to stretch her arms
to reach the subway straps. She's small!
Papa grins, "Hey, I'm six feet tall.
Watch me—I can reach the moon!"

My size? I'm still inching up.
When grown, will I be small or tall?
Mama says, "Whatever your height,
we know you'll measure up just right!"

Mama's hands are smooth and quick
at fixing zippers, tying bows.

Papa's hands are hard and large,
strong enough to boost me high.

My hands? Halfway in-between—
small and hard with rough-chewed nails.
Walking down the street at night,
holding hands feels just right!